Life Sutra

Life Sutra

Kumar Anu

ISBN 13: 978-93-89600-46-9

ATTENTION: SCHOOLS AND TEACHERS

This book is available at bulk discounts for educational purposes. Please contact kumar.anu@icloud.com for additional details.

Invincible Publishers

Registered Address: 201A, SAS Tower, Sector 38, Gurgaon - 122003

Phone - +91-124-4034247, +91 9355675555

www.invinciblepublishers.com

For Krishna.

Prologue.

The meaning of Life is to live. This Sutra has guided my life in good times and in bad times.

I have travelled the world in trains, planes, and automobiles. En route, I have spoken to hundreds of people about their philosophies in life. It was during one of these travels when I was introduced to the word—Sutra.

A Sutra is a sentence, a text, a set of words that guides a person's life. Everyone has a Sutra, a philosophy, or a way of life.

This book is a collection of one page stories of people from different walks of life. My research spans across rich people, poor people, spiritual people, and worldly people. Each person in this book has shared their Life Story and their Life Sutra.

The title of each story is a Life Sutra. You will connect with some Sutras and discard others. Whatsoever, every Sutra will give you a fresh perspective of life.

Kumar Anu

Dreams do come True.

Richa from London:

In kindergarten, a friend of mine showed me a doll that could talk, walk, and smile. She bought this doll from London. I was so fascinated by this beautiful doll that I could not sleep or eat for a week. I asked my parents to buy that doll for me—and—it was then when I understood the divide between the rich and the poor.

My parents were from a humble background. My father was a cab driver, and my mother was a nurse. They had invested all their savings in giving good education to their only daughter. There was no way that we could travel to London and buy that doll.

But my dreams never died. Every night, I used to dream that someone has constructed a bridge between India and London. I used to walk over that bridge to buy my doll. This dream became the most important part of my life. I was always excited to go to bed because that gave me an opportunity to dream about my dream.

Kumar Anu: So did you buy that doll?

Yes, I did. At the age of twenty-two, I was offered a job in London. It took me fifteen years to build my bridge, my dream. And I bought that doll with my father in London.

Search for your Path.

Ravi from the Himalayas, India:

In elementary school, I was told to listen to my teachers. In middle school, I was told to behave appropriately. In high school, I was told to study hard. In college, I was told to worry about my future. And I took all these suggestions, from the society— to my heart.

A few years later, I had everything—a good job, an apartment of my own, and a loving family. After all, I had worked hard all my life to achieve these milestones.

However, my soul was restless. I got tired of running the rat race. The need to maintain my status symbol, the nine-to-five job, and the retirement fund were taking a toll on me. One morning, I left my job, sold my apartment, and migrated to the mountains.

I bought an old house in the Himalayan foothills and converted it into a hotel. I make less money, but I am very happy. We homeschool our children and enjoy the serenity of the mountains.

Kumar Anu: Do you have a message for the restless souls out there?

Do not copy the behavior and customs of this world—instead—search for your own path.

Life is not about Money.

Kate from New York, United States:

I am a personal accountant for the rich and the famous. My job is to manage their daily spending, pay their bills, and do their errands. My clients are the billionaires and millionaires of New York City.

Kumar Anu: This sounds like an interesting job. Are you enjoying it?

No. I don't. I see a lot of suffering among rich people. And I want to change my job.

One evening, I saw this billionaire walk into his

room and close the wooden doors. A few minutes later, I could hear his tears and cries from my desk. He was lonely. His wife and kids were always busy shopping and socializing. They had no time for him.

That day, I understood the true meaning of happiness—it's not about money—it's about relationships.

Books can change your Life.

Veronica from Texas, United States:

I had a traumatic childhood. My parents were alcoholics, and after a few drinks, they would turn into monsters. They used to abuse each other, throw things at each other, and often hit each other.

During those tough years, I used to hide in a closet, cry for hours, and then fall asleep in pain. That closet was my hideout.

On the evening of my seventh birthday, as I was crying in the closet, something magical happened. A book of fairy tales fell from the top shelf into my lap. I read the entire night as Cinderella, Pocahontas, and Sleeping Beauty gave me hope.

After that day, my abusive parents never bothered me. I found peace in my books. Since then, I have read every book that gives hope. I believe that books are God's greatest gift to humanity.

Kumar Anu: What are your plans for life?

I am studying Literature at a University in Austin, Texas. After my education is completed, I am going to write a book for children that gives them hope, faith, and peace.

Don't Drink and Drive.

Jim from Dallas, Texas, United States:

My wife and I loved to party. Almost every weekend, we would dance for hours, drink beyond our limits, and sleep at odd hours. It was our lifestyle. As our kids became teenagers, we started taking them to these parties.

One night when my wife and I were completely drunk, I asked my fifteen-year-old daughter to drive us home. It was raining heavily, and the car toppled on the Dallas highway. None of us died, but we had multiple fractures.

My daughter was very scared when the cops arrived. She cried nonstop that night. Because she was in the driver's seat, she suffered the most. This incident went into government records and affected her college education.

It's been fifteen years now, and it was last month when the government agreed to issue her a driver's license.

Kumar Anu: Did this incident change you?

Our family has not touched alcohol since that accident.

Follow your Star.

Andy from Houston, Texas, United States:

I was seventeen years old, uneducated, and from a broken family. I started my first job as a laborer at a warehouse in Texas. My tasks were to load and unload the boxes from the delivery trucks.

One day, a top-level executive visited the warehouse. He drove a sports car, wore a costly suit, and spoke like a leader. He was in his early thirty's and attracted all the young women at the warehouse. His job, his style, and his education were the ingredients of his charisma.

I walked towards him and asked a simple question.

What have you done that makes you so special?

"I studied MBA from the best college in the country." He replied.

That day, I decided to become like him.

I joined the evening college and continued my job at the warehouse to fund my education. I worked hard in college and at the warehouse. I was determined.

As destiny played its game, ten years later, at the same warehouse, I was offered the same job as that executive.

Kumar Anu: Do you have a message for the dreamers out there?

Don't give up on your dreams. Find your star and follow your star.

A promise can change your life.

Steve from San Francisco, California, United States:

I was an alcoholic. My day started with a sip of whiskey. I carried the bottle to my work and would drink the entire day. In the evenings, I would open a new bottle to drink until mid-night. Whiskey was my life, and it was the only thing that gave me meaning.

But one day, everything changed. It was the day my daughter was born. I started drinking in the morning and almost drank for ten hours.

That night when I tried to hug my newborn, she turned away from me. The alcohol in my breath was monstrous to her soul. Her eyes looked at me through shame. I felt like she discarded me.

I could not handle that pain. I had to do something.

I joined the alcohol anonymous to get sober. It was tough, but I made it. Today is my daughter's seventeenth birthday, and it's also my seventeenth year without alcohol.

Kumar Anu: Do you have a message for those who struggle with alcohol?

The power of love can transform any addiction. Find someone you love and drop the beast of addiction from your life.

God has a plan.

Samar from New Delhi, India:

I was eight years old when my father, Devi Lal, was killed by the Pakistani Muslims. It happened right after the British announced the partition of India and Pakistan. My father was a Hindu Brahman Priest in our remote village, and our village got mapped with Pakistan.

When the Pakistani Muslims found out that I was the only son of Devi Lal, everyone was after my life. But destiny had other plans—Noora, a Pakistani Muslim, and a stranger to me, decided to become my savior.

Noora took me to his village and told everyone that

I was his relative. He even taught me some lines from the Quran so that my Hindu identity does not get revealed. After about a month, when things settled down, he dropped me at a refugee camp where I found my elder brother. We then migrated to India.

Kumar Anu: Are you in touch with Noora?

I have not seen Noora since the partition of India and Pakistan.

Love shows the Way.

Kathy from Paris, France:

I was the salesgirl at a shoe store. One evening a charming guy came to the store and kept trying different pairs of shoes. He spent three hours with me, talking about shoes, and eventually bought one pair.

He came the next day, and the next day, and every day for the next thirty days. I was his salesgirl. He bought one pair of shoes every day. Eventually, on the thirtieth day, he asked me out on a date.

On our first date, he told me that he had spent his entire monthly salary buying shoes. We laughed and got married in a few months.

Later we opened our own shoe store. We had to be in the shoe business because it was all about love.

Kumar Anu: Do you have a message for the lovers out there?

Love happens—you cannot do anything about it.

Old Age is Tough.

Bernie from Portland, Oregon, United States:

I am a doctor for the elderly. In medical terms, I am a geriatrician. At times, I have kept my patients alive for years, without emotions, and in a vegetative state.

Old age is tough—there is pain in the body, there are multiple medications, and above all, there is loneliness. I fail to understand that if parents can take care of their infants, why can't children take care of their aging parents? These old souls need love before they depart the world.

Kumar Anu: Has this profession transformed you?

I don't want to become a vegetable when I am ninety. I have signed a legal document that allows my lawyers to administer an assisted death for me. I can take a heavy dose of morphine and die at my will. And this can happen only in Oregon, United States.

Patience is the secret.

Jay from the Chicago, Illinois, United States:

It was my first day as a sales trainee. I was twenty-two years old and had learned everything about sales through my MBA from a prestigious college. But I had no real experience. My knowledge was based on books.

That day, at 9 AM, I was outside my manager's office. His assistant told me to wait. No one spoke to me until 2 PM, and then I was asked to keep waiting. Around 5 PM, the assistant told me that my manager was very busy, and he would see me the next day.

On day two, the same story was repeated, and I was asked to wait for one more day. On day three, I lost my patience and started complaining to his assistant. A few minutes later, my manager called me inside.

"Hello, Jay. I hope in the last three days you have learned the only skill required to be a successful salesman," He said.

"What is that?" I asked in complete frustration.

"Patience," He replied.

Kumar Anu: Wow! So do you practice patience with your clients?

This is my thirtieth year in sales, and patience has been the foundation of all my deals.

Life is a struggle.

Vijay from Jaipur, India:

I am an illegal immigrant. I came to the United States on a tourist visa and have been living here for the past ten years. I have not seen my family since I left India. My father died while I was working here.

Kumar Anu: Why are you doing this?

There was no money back home. It was tough. Now, I send money to my mother. She bought a house in Jaipur and helped my sister get married.

I work in a restaurant for twelve hours a day and earn everything in cash. I cannot drive because I cannot apply for a license. Life is not so easy, Sir.

I want to get married and settle in America. I have done enough for my family, and now I want to take care of myself.

Kumar Anu: Do you have a message for the strugglers out there?

Be nice to the waiters in the restaurants. We work hard for a good life.

Do not get Married to your job.

Daniel from New Jersey, United States:

My brother was an innovator, scientist, and workaholic. For twenty years, he worked for a fortune five company in New Jersey and developed many products for them.

However, last year, when the company was not doing well, he lost his job. He could not handle that pain. He thought that he was too old to start his life all over again. On a fateful night, he committed suicide.

Kumar Anu: What have you learned from him?

Enjoy your job, but don't get married to your job. Spend time with your family and friends—they are priceless.

Resolve your Guilts.

Kamal from Hyderabad, India:

At age ten, I did something wrong. I was jealous of my classmate, so I hid my pocket money in his lunch box. Later, I told my teachers that my money was stolen.

My classmate was caught and suspended for an entire month. This guilt stayed with me for the next 40 years. During those years, I often prayed and asked for the well-being of my classmate.

However, last month, I was unable to deal with this guilt anymore. So, I traveled to Hyderabad to seek forgiveness.

I found my classmate, told him the truth and asked for forgiveness.

He told me that, after that incident, he was very angry with God and stopped praying. But his life has been very good. He found success, fame, and fortune. He often felt that someone was praying for him.

Kumar Anu: What have you learned from this?

Prayers do work. Sometimes in strange ways.

Stop Complaining.

Biyu from Hong Kong:

My father took care of everything. Whenever I complained about life being unfair, he did everything possible to fix my life.

However, the real world was different. I started my first job in Hong Kong when I was twenty-one years old. My work was very painful—it was very political, my coworkers would make deals on my sales tips, and there was no one to help me. I went to my boss and started complaining left, right, and center. She listened to all of my complaints for an hour.

"I will take action on all of your complaints if you do one small thing for me," She said

"If you promise me that for the next twenty-one days, you will not complain about anything, I will do whatever you want me to do," She added.

I agreed and took the challenge very seriously. I never met my boss again to discuss this issue. After I stopped complaining, things started working for me. Instead of blaming the world for its problems, I started looking out for solutions.

Kumar Anu: Do you have a message for the whiners?

Stop complaining—it's a path for the escapists.

There is no Good Work or Bad Work.

Sahir from Chicago, Illinois, United States:

I was doing night shifts at our Chicago office. It was 10 p.m., and the office was quiet and serene. I was writing a software program when I saw a well-dressed man get out of his high-end sports car.

As I watched him through the tall windows of my office I promised myself, that one day, I will buy that car. After all, I had received my engineering and management degrees from prestigious colleges.

Surprisingly, the man from the sports car came into my office, put on his cleaning jacket, and started cleaning the floors. Yes, he was a cleaner with almost no education, but he probably made more money than I did.

Kumar Anu: What have you learned from this experience?

There is no good work or bad work. If you do your job with complete dedication—nothing can stop you from being successful.

Health is Wealth.

Raman from Delhi, India:

I am a salesperson. My job demands a lot—I travel five days a week, I eat out, and I am always worried about how to reach my sales goals. And yes, I do make a lot of money.

Last year, when my health took a toll on me, I visited a doctor in Delhi. After my examination, she said something that I will never forget.

"I do understand your mindset about being unhealthy—you think that instead of dying at eighty, you will die at seventy. So what difference does it make?" She said.

"However, let me assure you that if you don't take

care of your health now, your family will spend all of your hard-earned money to keep you alive until the age of eighty. I have no doubt that you will spend the last few years of your life in the hospital and almost bankrupt," she added.

Kumar Anu: What have you learned from her advice?

I try to stay healthy.

Get out of the Comfort Zone.

Augusto from Rio de Janeiro, Brazil:

At school, I was a backbencher. I never had the courage to say hello to my classmates. At work, I hardly spoke. I was comfortable at my desk writing software

Yes, I was an extreme introvert.

But a few years ago, everything changed at a corporate conference. I was challenged by a colleague of mine to speak to a few strangers sitting at a different table. That day, some heavenly power was working for me. I walked over to the strangers and spoke to them for an entire hour.

The following year, I took a sales job at my company. Over the years, I have sold computers worth five hundred million dollars. Before making any sales call, I always think of that day with the strangers. It gives me strength

Kumar Anu: What is the mantra of your life?

Fun begins when we leave our comfort zones.

Everyone needs love.

Sanjay from Punjab, India:

My mother died when I was twelve years old. A year later, my father remarried. My stepmom never accepted me, so I was asked to leave the house at age fifteen.

I was a hardworking student and was determined to make it big in life. I slept on the footpath, worked at a tea stall, and studied the judiciary at an evening college. After completing my studies, I found a job in the federal government. Today, I am the judge of a high court in India.

Last year, my father died, and I was informed about the cremation services. I met my stepmom and her two teenage sons, who were homeless and almost without money. I took care of them because I know the pain of being homeless.

Kumar Anu: You have a big heart!

I don't know about that, but I do know one thing—that everyone needs love.

Find a good heart.

Meera from Chennai, India:

India and Pakistan can never be friends. We Indians think that every problem in our country originates from our volatile neighbor. I have personally witnessed riots in India that are masterminded in Pakistan. And like many of my fellow Indians, I believed that Pakistanis didn't have hearts.

Strangely enough, I married a Pakistani.

I met him in America during my college days. He was an ordinary guy who loved music, who loved his family, and who wanted to live a better life. After numerous arguments in our classes, I understood that the common man, in both countries, is looking for peace. I learned that sometimes you have to choose love over hatred.

This hatred is created by politicians and religious fanatics living in Pakistan and India.

Kumar Anu: Do you want to say something to your fellow countrymen?

Don't judge a person by his country. There are good people everywhere. Find a good heart.

Goals will Change your Life.

Vova from St Petersburg, Russia:

Until grade four, I was a low IQ student. I could not focus on my classes, my books, and my studies. In my country, we rank students in each class. And for the previous two years, my rank was thirty—because—there were only thirty students in the class. It was as if my world was falling apart. But in grade five, I found the secret of success, that changed my life forever.

My parents sought the help of a life coach to transform my life. This life coach asked me to write—I am the topper of my class—one hundred times every day. However, I was not convinced about being the topper. I asked her if I could write—I rank fifth in my class—and she agreed. I wrote that goal every day for one year.

That year, I was ranked fifth in my class.

Something magical happens when we write out goals. The subconscious mind starts working on the goals, and we start doing things to achieve the goals. We activate our beliefs by writing our goals.

Kumar Anu: Have you used this strategy in your adult life?

It has been twenty-five years since that incident happened. And I have been writing my goals—one hundred times—every day. After I accomplish my goals, I create new ones. This is the only formula that guarantees success.

Everything is going to be OK.

Anup from Delhi, India:

In 1965, I was a student of engineering, and my monthly expenses were around one hundred rupees. One day, my one-hundred-rupee note was stolen.

I was upset for two days. I could not eat, sleep, or talk. The feeling of being helpless, the idea of spending the entire month without money, and the fear of informing my parents had completely destroyed my thinking ability.

On the third night, I got priceless advice from a

dear friend. He said, "Fifty years from now, you will laugh at this memory. So, why worry?"

Kumar Anu: What have you learned from this incident?

Take it easy. Everything is going to be OK.

Listen to the inner voice.

Ryan from Atlanta, United States:

My grandmother was my spiritual mentor. She always taught me to listen to my inner voice, and that God speaks to us through the silence of our hearts.

I live in Atlanta, which is approximately two hundred miles from my grandmother. One Saturday morning, my inner voice spoke to me very clearly and told me to visit my grandmother. However, I had plans for that night to party with my girlfriend.

I ignored my inner voice and stayed in Atlanta. My grandmother died that night while I was partying.

Kumar Anu: What have you learned from this?

Listen to the inner voice—it's the compass of our life. And I also pray to my grandmother to forgive me.

Life will knock you down.

James from San Francisco, United States:

I was an A+ student since kindergarten. I never believed in failures. It was my goal to get into an Ivy League school. I had prepared for it all my life.

However, I messed up my college board exams. When I came out of the exam, fear seeped into me. It felt like my dreams, my future, and my life was destroyed. I thought I would have to live my entire life as a failure.

That night, as I struggled with depression, I walked into my dad's room and started crying. He told me something that I have practiced all my life.

"Life knocks us down many times. But then, we get up and start working to fix things. If the results are good, we work hard to make them better. If our results are bad, we work hard to make them good. So, in reality, we are always working. Because life is not about our goals—it about the journey to our goals."

Kumar Anu: Do you apply this principle in your life?

I run a successful business in San Francisco. I have stumbled many times, but every time I failed, I got back up through hard work. I have no fear of failure.

Take care of your brother.

Dara from Cambodia:

My father pushed my brother and me from the top of the hill—to save our lives. The sounds of bullets and bombs were all around us. My country, Cambodia, was in the middle of a war between the communists and democrats. My father wanted to escape and cross over to Thailand for a better life.

As my brother, father, and I rolled down the hill, I saw a bullet hit my father in his heart. And before he took his last breath, he told me, "Run as fast as you can, and take care of your brother."

I took my younger brother on my shoulders and ran and ran. A few days later, we found ourselves in a church in Thailand. We found shelter and life, but we miss our father.

Kumar Anu: You are a strong man.

I was only thirteen years old when my father died. But since then, I have taken good care of my brother. I took my father's words to heart.

Clean the dishes or go to college.

Dave from Miami, Florida, USA:

As a teenager, I made wrong choices. I was hanging out with the street kids, I was smoking cigarettes, and I was bunking school. One night, I had a big argument with my father over school. I told him that I was not interested in studying, and I wanted to drop out. He tried to convince me, but that made me angrier. I threw the dinner plate at him, walked to my room, and slammed the door.

The next morning, my father told me that he was okay if I left school. However, to live in his house, I had to give him three hundred dollars every week. He took me to his friend's restaurant, and I was given a job to clean the dishes at the minimum wage.

I worked for the entire day and was dead tired. After working for a week in the restaurant, I had only twenty dollars left for myself. Life was miserable. That week, I realized the importance of education. And I told my father that I would go back to school

Kumar Anu: What do you do now?

I am a professor of sociology in Florida, United States. And I teach my students the importance of education.

One Mistake can Destroy your Life.

Willie from Dallas, Texas, United States:

We were pub-crawling in Dallas. I was just twenty-one years old and was officially allowed to drink. I can never forget that fateful night when I decided to drive back, at 3 a.m., with my girlfriend in the passenger's seat. I was completely drunk.

As we crossed a small bridge over the lake, I hit the barricades. The car crashed vertically, straight into the lake. My girlfriend took the impact on her skull. She went into a coma.

I could not forgive myself, and I prayed to God, with all of my heart and soul, to get her out of the coma. I promised God that I would never drink alcohol in my life. After I repented for eighteen months, God healed her, and she came out of the coma. This pain and suffering changed me for life.

Kumar Anu: How did it change you?

I became closer to God. And it's been twenty-three years since I have touched alcohol.

Fulfill your Duties.

Pritam from Delhi, India:

I never got the opportunity to go to school. My parents were daily-wage farmers. And in my village, education was limited to the rich and influential. At a very early age, I figured out that I would have to work hard to be successful. Hence, I migrated to Delhi in search of work.

I slept on the footpaths, did odd jobs, and joined a driving school. I cannot read or write, but I got my driver's license in a few months. Since then, I have been driving taxis all around Delhi. I work sixteen hours a day so that my children can go to school. I am trying to fulfill my dreams through my children.

Kumar Anu: Are your children proud of you?

I hardly see my children because of my odd working hours. But whenever I reach home, they greet me, hug me, and show me their school work. I cannot understand most of it, but I know that they love studying.

Life teaches Humility.

Mohan from Uganda:

I was born in Uganda. For two generations, my family built the most reputable diamond business in that country. We were blessed with fame, fortune, and success. We thought that we were not made for human struggle.

However, one morning in 1972, Idi Amin, the then president of Uganda, ordered the expulsion of all Indians. He said that he had a dream in which Allah had asked him to expel the Indian minority. All of our properties, bank accounts, and diamonds were confiscated. We were given ninety days to leave.

Our family of five landed in the United States as

refugees. We started doing small jobs at gas stations, grocery stores, and restaurants. We slept in shelter homes and struggled for months to make ends meet. Our pride, our reputation, and our ego were completely destroyed. We understood the truth of life.

Kumar Anu: How did this incident change you as a person?

It taught me humility. There is nothing certain in life. Be humble with the gifts of God.

Travel, Travel, Travel.

Brandon from Phoenix, Arizona, United States:

I am a sixty-year-old commercial pilot. I work for a courier delivery corporation in America. My job is to fly around the world to load and unload packages. I have stayed a day or two in every country on the map.

This job has given me perspective. In developing countries, I have met people who survive on minimum wages but are the happiest souls on earth. And in rich countries, I have met people who earn more than they can spend but are the most insecure souls on earth.

Kumar Anu: Do you have a message for the youngsters out there?

Travel Travel Travel —It gives you a true perspective on life.

Mistakes can Haunt you for Life.

Priya from Delhi, India:

For the past fifteen years, I have been working at a call center in Delhi, India. Every day, I talk to people from different countries, who speak different languages, and live in different time zones. I have become an expert in reading their minds and understanding their emotions. It's all about the tone of their voices—it reveals their secrets.

Two weeks ago, an old lady called me to buy a guitar for her daughter. I could feel a deep sense of pain in her voice. She kept talking about her daughter's desire to become a guitarist. As we spoke more, the tone in her voice revealed her loneliness. And before confirming the purchase, she said, "I hope my daughter likes this guitar because we have not spoken in twenty years."

Then she started crying and said, "Twenty years ago I left her with my husband and ran away with my boyfriend."

Kumar Anu: What is the best part of your job?

I get to comfort people, by the simple act of listening.

Save for your old age.

Jyoti from Kathmandu, Nepal:

I got married when I was sixteen. This was very common in the 1950s. I was an uneducated girl from a small town in Nepal. My husband was a hardworking man and had built a successful business in Kathmandu. I was the homemaker, and I took care of our three boys. We saved every penny to send our boys to private school. I wanted my kids to be educated.

However, things changed when my husband died. As he had no formal will, my children divided the inheritance among themselves. They told me that they would take care of me. I trusted them.

Now, I depend on my children for small things. They have their own families to take care of, and they feel that my expenses are a burden. The other day, I asked my eldest son to give me some money for new clothes.

"You already have so many saris. I don't have money to waste on useless things," My son, replied.

Kumar Anu: What is your message to the older people out there?

Love your kids. But save for your old age.

Learn to be the Eagle, not the Chicken.

Ron from New York, United States:

I was twenty-four when I joined the corporate world. My new job gave me everything—a workspace in Manhattan, a good salary, and a bunch of freshmen colleagues. We used to chat in conference rooms, break rooms, and hallways. My new world was filled with rumors and gossip. And then I met Dan.

Dan was the best coder in our company. His focus was his work. Whenever my colleagues started gossiping about Tom, Dick, and Harry not doing their work, Dan would walk away. In fact, we started gossiping about Dan and spreading rumors that he was not a professional. But Dan chose not to respond and let his work do the talking.

He was an eagle and could fly at a higher altitude. Whenever the chickens like us tried to pester him with office gossip, he would open his wings and take the higher path

It's been twenty years since we joined. I am still a coder, and Dan is the director of our company.

Kumar Anu: This teaches a lot.

If you want to be on the other side of the curtain, you've got to become an eagle.

It's difficult to be Human.

Freddy from Austin, Texas, United States:

I was a meat lover. I used to go to the grocery store every day to buy my favorite meats—the juicy chicken, the sliced pork, or the fresh goat. In the United States, meat products are hygienically wrapped and sold like precious gems. Until age fourteen, I never thought about the animal being killed to feed me.

However, a family reunion in Mexico changed my perception of meat. We decided to cook a goat for dinner, and I went with my cousins to buy the meat from a butcher. The butcher had live goats in his shop, and he asked us to select a goat.

My eldest cousin picked a healthy goat, but then the butcher told us to pick a younger one for juicy meat. He pointed us toward a younger goat. The baby goat got terrorized. But then the butcher took his knife and slit its throat. The infant goat died in front of me. And when the goat's blood stopped flowing, the butcher cleaned the carcass and packed it for us.

Kumar Anu: Looks like you have a very soft heart.

I cried that night. But I do understand that this is the reality of life.

Learn to validate Life.

Linda from London, United Kingdom:

I have lived in denial for the first fifteen years of my life. I had the best image of my parents. They did everything possible, within their means, to give us a good life. My father worked hard to send us to the best school in London, my mother was an organized homemaker, and above all, my parents never fought. There were no arguments in our house. We were a perfect family.

It was my sixteenth birthday, and we were getting ready to go out for dinner. My parents asked my brother and me to wait in the living room, and they locked themselves in another room. After two hours of waiting, I walked to their door and started listening to their conversation.

I could hear crying, physical abuse, and an ugly argument. It sounded like they would kill each other. I got so scared that I went and hugged my little brother. That night, I understood that my family was not perfect—my parents were doing an excellent job of hiding the truth.

Kumar Anu: How did this incident change you?

I am a mother of two beautiful daughters, and I share everything with them. Telling the truth helps them validate life. It saves them from being in denial.

Sacrifice for Good Life.

Mary from Vietnam:

I was born during the Vietnam War. There were bombs, gunfire, and bloodshed everywhere. In Vietnam, my parents struggled for food, water, and even life itself. They were looking for ways to get out of the war-torn country.

When I was ten, my parents put me into a boat with two hundred people to help me leave Vietnam. This boat was operated by smugglers, and my parents could afford the price for only one passenger. They decided to send their only daughter. They gave me a few cans of tuna fish, a bottle of water, and a note. The note had my name, my parents' names, and a prayer to keep me safe. I have not seen my parents since then.

I landed in a migration camp, and from there, I was adopted by an American family. They became my foster parents. I went to school and then to college and found a job. But there has not been a single day when I haven't thought about my parents in Vietnam. I cannot comprehend their pain when they decided to put me on that boat.

Kumar Anu: Your story has touched my heart.

My search is on, and I hope to find them one day.

Find your Calling.

Lee from Hong Kong:

At age ten, I used to save my pocket money to buy stationery from a manufacturing unit—pencils, notebooks, craft paper—anything that I could sell at my school. I am not from a poor family; on the contrary, my parents had surplus money to give us a good life. I just had the soul of an entrepreneur.

During my teen years, I bought tons and tons of raw almonds at throwaway prices. With the help of a few friends, we exported the almonds to Indonesia. We made a killing, and I was able to fund my college education with that money.

I was born to be in the trading business. My soul can sense opportunities, requirements, and market potential. My passion has motivated me to build the best trading company in Hong Kong.

Kumar Anu: What is the most essential skill required to be in trading?

Building relationships. Profits are a byproduct.

Become Color Blind.

Divya from Charleston, South Carolina, United States:

We migrated to the United States when I was thirteen years old. It's tough for a teenage girl to make new friends in a new country. In India, everyone in my school had the same skin color, came from a similar economic background, and we were all Indian.

But my new school in Charleston was different. There was a clear demarcation in my class—the white kids and the black kids. They did not accept the brown kids. The white kids thrashed me and asked me to stay with the blacks. And the black kids humiliated me and asked me to go back to my brown land of snake charmers.

But then I used my expertise in math to bridge the divide between blacks and whites. My class was struggling with math, and my teacher asked me to help other kids. I went out of my way to help both the black kids and the white kids. And because of spending time with each other, we understood life and friendship beyond our skin color.

Kumar Anu: So, do you have both black and white friends?

I am color blind towards my friends. I look at the heart—that is beyond white, black, or brown.

Take Risks in Love and in Life.

Pedro from Brasilia, Brazil:

I loved her from the core of my heart. We were studying computer engineering in Brazil. She was the most beautiful girl on earth—black hair, glowing eyes, and an infectious smile. Everything about her was mesmerizing. But, I never had the courage to propose to her.

I was afraid of being rejected, of being stupid, and of losing her friendship. So I did nothing. On the other hand, my roommate was a very clear thinker.

He fell in love with the same girl, and proposed her at the right time. They married a few years later.

I cried on their wedding day. But I also learned the biggest lesson of my life—it's better to take risks than to have regrets. She might have said no if I had proposed to her, but at least I would have expressed my love. And maybe she would have said yes.

Kumar Anu: Have you conquered your fears now?

I manage a hedge fund, and my strength is my ability to take risks. I have learned this the hard way—by losing the love of my life.

Smoking Kills.

Chetan from Calcutta, India:

Anand and I did everything together—bunking classes, falling in love with the same girl, and smoking cigarettes. We shared our cigarettes and fought for the last puff. He used to say, "Whoever gets the last puff will live longer." At that time, I had no idea that we would struggle for our lives.

I migrated to the United States when I was nineteen, and we lost touch. In the 1970s, there were no mobile phones, no e-mail, and no social media.

Nevertheless, my smoking continued. And every

time I took the last puff, I thought about Anand.

Last year, I was diagnosed with stage one lung cancer. I think I will survive. In the hospital, I thought about Anand. I tried to contact him but had no success. Last month, out of the blue, Anand's mother called me. She told me that Anand died from lung cancer twenty years ago. His last wish was that I would quit smoking.

Kumar Anu: Do you have a message for smokers?

Smoking kills. It's written on every pack of cigarettes.

Find your Spiritual Life.

Aditya from Mumbai, India:

I have two lives. In my earthly life, I am a software programmer working for a multinational in Mumbai. In my spiritual life, I am a singer. I sing in my house, in my car, and in the streets. It brings me divine peace.

I was trained to write software so that I could make a living. I did all the regular stuff that society demands—got a job, got married and raised my kids. Every day, I code for eight hours, and I spend two hours with my family. But beyond that, my life is all about music. My singing connects me with the creator of the universe—after all, our vocal cords are directly connected to our hearts.

Kumar Anu: What is your greatest reward?

The other day, I started singing in the metro. People were scandalized; they had never seen a person in an office suit singing on a train. But then my voice started attracting them, and I got a standing ovation. That was worth more than my paycheck.

Find your Mentor.

Simran from Agra, India:

My mother wanted to become a professional Kathak dancer. But in the India of the 1950s, women were supposed to get married by age 18 and take care of their husbands. My mother buried her dreams the day she got married.

However, things changed the day I was born. When she nursed me for the first time, she made a decision that I would become the world's best Kathak dancer.

Growing up, I had a tough schedule. My mother woke me up at 4 a.m. and watched my practice each and every day. She was a taskmaster. I was served breakfast only after I completed my physical workout. I believe it was her determination that made me India's best Kathak dancer.

Kumar Anu: Do you think you would have been successful without her?

Behind every successful person, there is someone else. I was blessed to have a mother who changed my destiny. And in the process, she fulfilled her dreams.

Your Ego can Destroy your Life.

Vadim from Moscow, Russia:

My father was my hero. I wanted to be like him. He was a good husband, a good parent, and the world's best businessman. He built his business from a humble background. He designed Russia's indigenous telecom system. He groomed me to join his business.

But things took an ugly turn when I started working with my father. I had a disagreement with him on our marketing strategy. I wanted to put more funds into advertising, and he wanted to put the funds into product development. In a heated argument, he told me that I was good for nothing and asked me to leave the business.

That night, I left my business, my family, and my

hero. I moved out of Russia and started my own life. I had no contact with my father. The ego within me was bigger than our relationship. Ten years later, I learned that he died of a heart attack.

Kumar Anu: Do you regret your decision?

I cry every night. I miss him. Our egos destroyed our lives.

Learn to take Tough Decisions.

Deepak from Bangalore, India:

I was in ninth grade when my father told me that if he gets hospitalized in future and the doctors put him on life support —I will have to make a decision to let him go. That night, I gave him a promise that I would not keep him alive on a life-support system.

Twenty years later, he was hospitalized for a blood clot in his brain. Within a few hours, his kidneys failed and he was put on life support. The doctors told us that there was still hope, but he was in a lot of pain.

My entire family, including my distant relatives, came to visit. In India, people love to give advice. And everyone was against my decision to remove the life-support system. Some told me that I would carry the burden of killing my father. Letting him die has been the toughest decision of my life.

Kumar Anu: Are you at peace with your decision?

My entire family has disowned me. But deep in my heart, I know that my father is very proud of me.

My Wife is My Hero.

Rahul from Bihar, India:

My wife was illiterate and uneducated. But her story is an example of persistence and hard work.

I come from a tribal family in rural India. Because I was from the only rich family in the community, I got the opportunity to leave Bihar, India, and study agriculture in the United States. The day I graduated, my parents wanted me to get married. In my community, arranged marriages are not an option but a norm. My parents arranged my marriage. I spoke to my wife for the first time after our marriage ceremony was completed.

The next week, I came back to America with my illiterate wife. However, she surprised me with her confidence and desire to learn and explore the new world around her. She asked me to teach her one sentence in English every day. And day by day, she persisted. She mastered the language within a year.

Kumar Anu: Do you still teach her English?

It's been five years since we got married. She speaks flawless English and manages the customer support for my agricultural business in the United States.

There is only one God.

Adam from New York, United States:

My father is a Muslim from Pakistan. He migrated to the USA for higher education. He is a devoted follower of Islam. He met my mother in college. She is a devout catholic of Spanish origin from Argentina.

Yes, love has no barriers.

Both of them continued to practice their religion after marriage. We had a Bible and a Quran sitting next to each other in our small prayer room. My father practiced *Namaz* five times a day. And my mother prayed to the Lord in the morning. They believed in God, but religion was never discussed openly.

Last year, on my thirteenth birthday, my parents asked me to choose one religion. They explained the philosophies of both Islam and Christianity.

Kumar Anu: And what did you choose?

I am still evaluating. All I understand is that there is one God.

Parenting is the Toughest Job.

Kalpana from Surat, India:

Homemaker, cook, cleaner, and the mother of three—my mom often lost her peace of mind. She was the lady dictator of our house. She had advice for everything—what to wear, what to eat, and what to say. She had no control over her anger and often slapped me. It's very common in India to get spanked by your mom.

I often told my mom that I would leave the house as soon as I turn eighteen. And if I had children of my own, I would raise them in peace and become a better mom than she was to me.

However, my perspective completely changed when I gave birth to twin boys. They are high-energy kids, and it's difficult to manage them. Becoming a mom made me realize what my mom went through. She worked 24/7 for her children and tried to raise us to be responsible adults.

Kumar Anu: Are you a better parent than your mom?

Never ask that question to a mom. The truth is that every mother is a nurturer by heart, and we do many things in the background that no one sees.

Look at the Big Picture.

Deepak, from Punjab, India:

When I was a high schooler in Punjab, India, my father gave me an advice that changed the perspective of my life. His advice influenced my thinking process, his advice brought focus into my life, and his advice is the reason for my success.

He said, work hard for two years, in high school, and enjoy life for the next twenty years. He taught me to see—the Big Picture.

While my friends were skipping classes, dating girls, and drinking beer, I was studying hard to get into a good college. I understood deep inside my heart that if I work hard in high school, and get into a good college—my life will be transformed, and it surely did.

I got admission into one of the best business schools, and after graduating I found a high paying job. And then, I started celebrating life, dating girls, and drinking beer.

On the contrary, my classmates struggled for jobs, their girlfriends left them for better prospects, and they don't have money to buy few rounds of beer.

Kumar Anu: Do you evaluate long-term consequences in all your decisions?

Yes. My thinking process is always looking for long-term rewards. People look at short-term benefits and then suffer in life. However, I have understood that if you want to succeed, look at—the Big Picture.

Morning has gold in its mouth.

Roshan from New Delhi, India:

My past life had the following morning rituals—get up at 8 a.m., grab a cup of tea, read newspapers, surf the internet, respond to chat messages, and update my social media status. After about an hour of consuming myself with the world, I used to get ready and leave for my job at a multinational corporation.

However, I started noticing that I was not growing professionally. I was unable to give a hundred percent to my job. My focus was always distorted. And I was lost in unwanted thoughts.

Then, one day, my grandmother shared with me an old German proverb—Morning has gold in its mouth.

For reasons unknown to me, this proverb got immersed into my soul. And I understood that my thoughts, during the morning hour, were contaminated. I was allowing newspaper negativity to dominate my thoughts. I was allowing social media friends to dominate my thoughts. I was allowing the outside world to dominate my thoughts.

I decided to feed better thoughts into my morning hour. I realized that the morning hour could guide my entire day towards contentment. And after changing my morning rituals, within a few months—I was transformed. I found professional success.

Kumar Anu: How do you spend your morning hour after the transformation?

In my present life—I do not touch my mobile phone during the first hour. I do not read newspapers in the morning. I journal three pages about my life goals. I list down the essential tasks for the day. And above all, I connect with the divine, during the first hour, with prayer and meditation.

Find Dignity.

Rajan from Jaipur, India:

I was an accountant working for the government. I had a routine that I was following religiously—wake up at 6 AM, arrive at work by 9 AM, and leave work by 5 PM. There was an order in my daily life. My work gave me dignity, purpose, and, most importantly, routine.

However, last year, by the stroke of good luck or bad luck, I got some inheritance money from a distant relative that had died unexpectedly. This money was enough to take care of my family for the next fifty years. I thought that I found freedom. And as destiny had planned it, I resigned from my government job.

This was the worst decision of my life—I lost focus and became lazy. The routine and order of daily life was lost. Also, my wife, a dedicated homemaker, was jobless. She had no daily tasks to do—she got a cook to prepare our food, a cleaner to clean the house, and a helper to buy groceries. The money in our bank was working for us.

We lost our dignity. Dignity comes only with the work we do. There is an old saying in India that says that "Work is Worship". And we lost our Worship. We were not earning our bread.

Kumar Anu: So, what are you doing to fix this mess in your life?

I am back to my old job. And my wife is a homemaker again. I work for dignity and she takes care of the family for self-respect.

Believe me, we are nothing without the work we do.

Giving is Receiving.

Veer from USA:

My father migrated to the USA when I was five years old. The day we arrived in this beautiful country—we had one hundred dollars in our pocket, four bags, and six illiterate family members.

My father worked sixteen hours a day, at gas stations, grocery stores, and restaurants to provide shelter and food for us. We were always short of money— skipping meals, sharing clothes, and walking miles every day. In those early years, I was very angry with my father that he did not have enough money to take care of my wishes.

One evening, on my 16th birthday, I discussed money with my father. It was a heated argument, and he told me that—he has taken good care of his family, that he is very contented with his minimal belongings, and, all his life, he was donating ten percent of his income to charities.

That night I completely lost it. How could he donate when we were so poor? I could have done so much with that donated money. During that heated conversation, he told me one thing that got stuck in my memory forever. He said, "My needs are limited; therefore, I help others in need."

Kumar Anu: Did his philosophy influence your philosophy in life?

I stored my anger against him for many years. I wanted to become a rich man, so I started my own business, worked hard, and became a millionaire at the age of thirty.

However, when I got all the money in the world, and yet, struggled to find contentment in life. I realized that— my needs are limited; therefore, I need to help others in need.

I became just like my father.

I understood that it is in giving that we receive.

Rise above the problem.

Nikita from Moscow, Russia:

I love cooking—it's my hobby, my passion, and my mediation. When I cook, my mind shuts off completely. I can be my true self. But the biggest reward of my passion is that it helps me look at my problems from a fresh perspective.

The other day, I was unable to decode a computer virus for a high-profile client in Russia. I am a software programmer, and I help corporate customers keep their computers safe. This is a high- pressure job, and, on that particular day, I was under immense stress. That night at home, I decided to cook Pad Thai.

In the process of cleaning the meat, cutting the vegetables, heating the oil, and adding the spices, my mind became completely quiet. I was in my own world. I forgot about my job and the virus. And before I ate my first bite, I had a terrific idea—out of nowhere—to debug and kill the virus.

Kumar Anu: So, cooking is the secret of your success?

You can never solve a problem at the level of the problem—you have to rise above it.

Find Work-Life Balance.

Tony from Houston, Texas, United States:

On a busy Monday morning in Houston, I found blood all over our office restroom. A colleague of mine was on the floor. He was not breathing, and his pulse had stopped. He had a massive heart attack. I called 911, and the ambulance arrived in a few minutes.

At the hospital, the doctors managed to revive him and placed him on life support. But after about a month's struggle, his family decided to let him go and disconnected the life support.

That month, everyone talked about him. Some said that he was a chain smoker, some said he was overly ambitious, and some said that he had anger issues. But for me, he was a common man from a humble background. He worked hard for 32 years to give a good life to his family. He was a dedicated salesman. He had spent his life's savings on his retirement home and was looking forward to collecting the keys next week.

Kumar Anu: Have you changed after his death?

I have understood that life is short—and we have to practice work-life balance.

Do not feed the Bad Wolf.

Etu from Sedona, Arizona, USA:

During my teenage years, I had angst against, my mother, my father, my teachers, the American government, and anyone who did not agree with me. I was a difficult child, but those adolescent years have taught me a lot about happiness.

Once I threw my food on the floor, showing disrespect to my mother. It was my way of telling her that I am very angry with life. And I still remember her words that changed my life forever:

"Don't let the anger feed the bad wolf inside you."

Growing up in the native American culture, I was taught about the presence of bad wolf and good wolf inside every human being. The bad wolf is the egoic mind and the good wolf is the spiritual mind.

The egoic mind feeds itself on fear, guilt, and anger. It's fearful about the future ahead of us, it's guilty about the mistakes made in the past, and it's angry about the present moment.

The spiritual mind feeds itself on love, peace, and forgiveness. It sees love as the essence of life, it sees peace as a state of happiness, and it sees forgiveness as the force to dissolve the egoic mind.

Kumar Anu: How do we access that spiritual mind?

To access the spiritual mind, you have to dissolve the egoic mind. This is not an easy task and the human race has been trying to do this for ages.

However, a good place to start will be to let go of the fear, guilt, and anger inside you. Every time you recognize these negative emotions, drop them right away. This is done through the power of will.

The next step is to feed the spiritual mind with love, peace, and forgiveness. As your spiritual mind grows, it will dissolve the egoic mind on its own.

Happiness is hard work.

Always question, Is this my best work?

Rosa from Aguascalientes, Mexico:

Growing up, I had a dream of writing a bestselling book. I had learned the skills, of good writing, in high school. But, writing a book was like climbing Mount Everest. I was short of will power. Whenever I had time to write—I would procrastinate—thinking that I do not have the skills to write a bestseller.

For a good part of my life, I buried my dream and continued with my daily activities. However, through this thing called 'destiny', I met a painter at an art exhibition who changed my life forever.

This painter was sketching his artwork, then erasing it, and then sketching it all over again. As I started observing him—he did the same thing again and again—sketching, erasing, sketching.

My critical mind started laughing at him. The mind had many questions—why is he doing this? After all, he made a reasonably good sketch. He did not have to erase it.

With the intention of making fun of him, I

approached him and asked, "Sir, why are you erasing a good sketch and starting it all over again?"

And his answer enlightened my mind and my heart forever.

"This is the only thing that separates me from regular artists. This is the only thing that brings out my best creation. And this is the only thing that helps me sell my sketches for a million dollars. Every time, I draw something, I ask myself—is this my best work? If the answer is a 'no', then, I erase it and start it all over again." He replied.

Kumar Anu: And how did this help you in your life?

His message sunk into my soul. I started working on my book, and every day, after my writing was completed, I asked myself—is this my best work? If the answer was "no", then I started all over again.

As of today, I have published ten books and seven of them are bestsellers. The credit of my success goes to the artist in that exhibition, who taught me how to create a masterpiece.

The answer is in the hormones.

Sam from Colombo, Sri Lanka:

Happiness is a state of mind. Happiness is all about the hormones like dopamines, endorphins, and serotonins. These hormones keep us happy. And they are produced by the body.

We, human beings, are looking for happiness at wrong places—the house we own, the car we drive, the movie we watch, the job we do, the hobbies we have, and the people we have around us.

Seriously, do you think these external elements can deliver happiness? I don't think so.

Kumar Anu: And how can the body produce the hormones like dopamines, endorphins, and serotonins?

The path to happiness starts with regular exercise and a healthy diet. It's that simple—what you do with your body and what you feed to your body.

Exercise thirty minutes every day and you will become a happy person for no reason. Eat fresh vegetables every day and you will become a blissful person for no reason. Your body will overflow with dopamines, endorphins, and serotonins. These two recipes work better than any other happiness drug.

Follow your own path.

Marco from Rio Salvador, Brazil:

My best friend is an entrepreneur. He is a manufacturing genius, and he has made millions of dollars. He is very passionate about his work.

I was envious of him. I wanted to be like him—

have my own business, be my own boss, and make lots of money.

I started a toy manufacturing company and failed miserably. Then, I jumped into the restaurant business and failed again. I lost everything, and today I am surviving on food stamps.

As a child growing up in Brazil, I wanted to fly the world as a pilot. I wish I had followed my dream.

Kumar Anu: What have you learned from all of this?

The secret of life—it is better to follow your own path than to struggle on someone else's path.

Happiness is Cleanliness.

Neelima from Chennai, India:

People tell me that I have a disorder—OCD—obsessive compulsive disorder. I am crazy about keeping my house clean. My natural instincts drive me to put things in order.

My living room breathes fresh air because there is not a single particle of dust on the couch. My kitchen is at peace because the dishes are washed immediately after use. And my bedrooms are well dressed because the blankets are folded first thing in the morning.

I spend two hours every day to clean my house.

People often make fun of me; they have called me psycho and have asked me to visit a doctor. But no one understands that this OCD is my meditation. All said, meditation is all about being in the present moment—and my OCD keeps me in the present moment. It quiets my mind.

Kumar Anu: Do you find contentment, satisfaction, and happiness after two hours of cleaning?

Happiness is a state of mind. And cleaning changes my state of mind. It brings me one step closer to happiness.

Keep your Promises.

Giri from Delhi, India:

I got into cigarettes at age fourteen. I used to hang out with my neighborhood gang, and all the boys smoked. I was the last one to light the cigarette in my mouth. But I had to do this—otherwise—I would have become an outcast in my own group.

Smoking gave me dignity, style, and charisma. The girls looked at me as if I was a hero, an icon, and an adult. Every inhalation of that tobacco wrapped in paper, give me a kick for a few minutes—I loved it.

However, a year later, my mother saw me smoking. She got very upset and cried for a month. At that stage of my life, I was in love with only two things—cigarettes and my mom. And I got very disturbed, when I saw my mom crying.

She asked me to give her a vow that I will never

ever smoke. Now, vows are a big thing in my culture. If I took the vow and do not fulfill it, karma could do bad things to my mom.

I resisted taking the vow. But over the next few days, I was heartbroken to see my mom crying. Hence, in an act of love and desperation—I promised her that I will never ever smoke in my life.

Kumar Anu: Did you keep your promise?

The initial months were tough; I had palpations, anxiety, and depression. But I got over it. It has been ten years, and I have not touched that beast. For me, it's all about keeping my promise. It's about integrity.

Follow your Heart.

Jose from Mexico City, Mexico:

My father is a humble mechanic who owns a small auto shop. My best memories of childhood are playing with my father in his auto shop. During my teenage years, my father was always available to solve my emotional issues. He was my best friend until I moved out of Mexico City to pursue my dreams.

I became the account manager of a Fortune 500 company and was responsible for the revenue of seventy million dollars. I was traveling the world, I had won the employee-of-the-decade award, and I was nominated to become the CEO of the company.

But my soul was very restless.

are attached, the more you suffer.

Detachment, on the other hand, is living on the edge. A coin has three sides—heads, tails, and the edge. If head is success, profit, or joy. And tail is failure, loss, or suffering. Then edge is the seat of detachment. Bhutanese people live on the edge. We understand that duality is a part of life and embrace life on the edge.

Kumar Anu: And how do I learn detachment?

Detachment is an art and can be learned only through practice. You have to train your mind to live on the edge.

That is the secret of Bhutan—the happiest country in the world.

Go back to your Good Memories.

Roberto from New York, United States:

I am seventy- five years old, and I have experienced almost everything—birth, death, and life itself. We humans go through the cycle of suffering and joy. It's inevitable. And like many other human beings, at times, I do go through depression. It is my karma.

However, I found an antidote for my depression.

Whenever I am lonely or sad, I travel back to my adolescent years. I look at the pictures of my youth. There is something magical in those years—the first love, the first kiss, and the first girlfriend.

Those memories of youth are my comfort zone. They heal me faster than any other drug.

Kumar Anu: Do you have a message for the youngsters out there?

Make good memories in your teen years. They bring happiness when you get old.

Everything is going to be okay.

Elizabeth from Rio de Janeiro, Brazil:

Last year, my only son died. He took his last breath while he was in my arms. His last words were, "Mom, everything is going to be okay."

For parents, the toughest part of life is seeing their children die. I had prayed to the almighty with my heart and soul to take my life and let him live. But I guess his journey was over. And to my surprise, the silent minutes after his last breath changed my life forever.

I felt sadness, pain, and suffering for a few

And after ten years in the corporate world, I decided to return to my family. And I decided to work with my father. I make less money, but life is great, and I am happy and thankful to be with my father. The best part of my day is when I sit down, for a cup of coffee, with my father, and that brings me immense joy.

Kumar Anu: Do you miss the corporate life?

Not at all. Life is not about money or success. It is about family.

Let Go and Let Life.

Hong Li from Bangkok Thailand:

My father died last week, and I have moved on with my job, my children, and my life. That is how we do it in Thailand. We practice something called—*mai pen ka*—it means to let go and let life. We don't worry, we don't think a lot, and we laugh at our struggles. This practice makes Thailand one

Kumar Anu: So, you don't cheat anymore?

Everyone on planet earth is suffering. It's a collective pain. And the truth is that —we can find happiness only by serving others.

Hence, in an effort to clear my bad karma, I started practicing compassion towards my friends, and my countrymen. Instead of becoming a money maniac, I started helping them.

My mantra has been simple—help one person every day, through service, through money, or through emotional counseling. You have to experience compassion to understand the joy of helping others.

When you do something for a fellow human being with a pure heart—you are not helping that person, instead, you are helping your soul to grow.

It is transformative. It is the birthplace of happiness.

Walk. Talk. Laugh.

Remo from New York, USA:

My life in New York City was taking a toll on me. Getting up early, taking the subway to work, eating lunch in my office cube, working for ten hours, coming home dead tired, eating pre-cooked food, and having sleepless nights.

I decided to change the scenery of my life and travel to an unknown city. I packed my bags for a hiking trip to Ladakh, India.

As I hiked through a small village in the Ladakh valley, I saw a group of women walking, talking, and laughing. They were making fun of each other, enjoying the weather, and talking about the hikers in the valley. Their faces were glowing, and their smiles clearly indicated how happy they were.

These women belonged to a lower-middle-class

of the happiest countries in the world.

Kumar Anu: What about the grieving period? Don't you miss your father?

Our grieving period is a few days. We understand that the opposite of Death is Birth. But there is no opposite of Life. We have to live.

Find joy in doing simple things.

Aaron from Malaysia:

Last year, I had an *ah-ha* moment that changed the perspective of my life.

I am forty years old, working as an accountant in Malaysia. All my friends talk about doing big things like—finding your passion, making the world a better place, and having a mission in life. They are all influenced by inspirational videos on social media. They get motivated by these so-called

Inspirational Gurus.

These conversations with my friends made me very restless. I felt like I was wasting my life and living like an animal without a purpose.

But I had no desire to make the world a better place. This might sound selfish, but it is true.

Last year, I realized that, only if I am happy—I can make everyone around me happy. Hence, I started looking at things that bring me happiness.

I found five things—eating good food, sleeping well, talking to people, practicing yoga every day, and praying in the presence of God. These are simple things and do not require skills or money.

I decided to enjoy these daily activities.

Kumar Anu: These are basic human activities.

I enjoy life in doing simple things—that is the secret of happiness for me.

Take it easy.

Brenda from Washington, United States:

I am celebrating my one hundredth birthday today with my great-grandchildren in Washington. This generation is very restless and scared about their future. They are worried about terrorism, about nuclear bombs, and about unknown diseases.

I have seen it all—the good times and the bad times. I have seen two world wars, I have seen people dying from hunger, and I have seen people suffering from leprosy and polio.

But then, I also saw that humanity survived the world wars, made significant progress in fighting world hunger, and developed a free vaccine for leprosy and polio.

Kumar Anu: Do you have a message for the world on your hundredth birthday?

Every generation goes through the turmoil of fear and insecurity. Do not worry; everything is going to be okay. Just chill!

Detachment is the Secret.

Pema from Bhutan:

A few years ago, I visited the United States and was very surprised to see so many unhappy people. The citizens of the richest country in the world live with the insecurities of life—fear of losing their jobs, fear of failed relationships, and fear of old age.

In Bhutan, we practice detachment in our day-to-day lives. And that is the secret of our happiness.

The root cause of all the suffering in life is attachment. This attachment to people, places, and things bring dissatisfaction in life. The more you moments. But then, holding his dead body in my arms, I felt grace all over me. I experienced the presence of God. Underneath the pain, I found deep peace, rest, and the cleansing of my soul.

I have not cried since he died. I moved on with life and migrated to Brazil to work with the Red Cross. My relatives think that I was not a loving mother. But, they have not experienced the peace that came with my suffering.

Kumar Anu: How do you help patients at the Red Cross?

I pass on my son's message—Mom, everything is going to be okay.

Deb from New Delhi, India:

For five years, I worked on a prototype that could change the way we produce solar electricity in India. I was in desperate need of a federal grant. Without government support, my invention would be a waste. I did all the paperwork, provided the necessary approvals, and submitted my prototype to the government.

But the approving officer was very rude, grumpy, and unkind. On my first visit, he told me there was no grant available, but I could check back again in a few months. On my second visit, he said, "Don't waste your time here. The government does not have money for this useless stuff."

Heartbroken and directionless, I decided to pray the night before my last visit to the government office. I asked God almighty to send the right people into my life. And my life was transformed the next day.

It turned out that the grumpy officer was on vacation that day, and his manager was filling in. This person was very friendly and passionate about my project. After I demonstrated my project for an hour, he approved my grant right way. And to my surprise, he gave me permanent access to the government lab.

Kumar Anu: Wow, Prayers do work!

Yes. A heartfelt prayer is the secret of my happiness.

Travel can change your Life.

Laura from Phoenix, Arizona, United States:

My father died on my 18th birthday. I struggled every day to deal with his loss. My mother suggested that I go on a backpacking trip from the east coast to the west coast of the United States. This three-month-long trip changed my life forever.

I met people from all walks of life—single parents who were raising their children, students who were working in gas stations to pay off their college education, farmers who worked sixteen hours a day to feed their families, homeless drug addicts who regretted the choices they made, and lonely people who had no families.

Kumar Anu: Looks like travel gave you a fresh perspective on life.

My suffering felt small compared to others who had suffered so much. I was able to move on with my life.

Find your Religion.

David from Dover, Delaware, United States:

Growing up in an orthodox Hindu family, I was always overwhelmed with the outdated, superstitious, and confusing concepts of Hinduism.

I was in search of a religion that could deliver permanent happiness. And I found my answer in Christianity. After speaking to a world-famous pastor—I found peace in Jesus Christ. I understood that Christianity is the religion of happiness. I got baptized and changed my name to David.

However, to my surprise, a colleague of mine who was raised as a devout catholic had embraced the Hindu Hare Krishna movement. He told me that the Bible was very confusing, and the Bhagavad Gita (the sacred book of Hindus) had answers for all of life's problems. I believe that he has lost his mind.

Kumar Anu: Do you believe that there are two Gods—one for Hindus and another for Christians?

No answer. There was complete silence.

Happiness is freedom.

Baris from Istanbul, Turkey:

The walk from my school to my home was twenty minutes. And those twenty minutes were the best part of my life. I witnessed life on the streets of Istanbul—food vendors, bikers, old people, young lovers, and many others. I also met Fakira, who changed the perspective of my life.

Fakira was an artist who sold his paintings on the streets. He was a crazy traveler and had backpacked on all seven continents. The highlight of my day was listening to his stories and his adventures. Once, he told me that life is a romance for those who have a free spirit.

My encounters with Fakira made me understand that we have a choice of being free. At that young age, I decided to live my life in freedom—so that I can do things I want to do, disown the traditions of this world, and follow my dreams.

Kumar Anu: And how exactly are you living a free life?

I have lived my life on my terms. I never married. I have many friends, but I spend a lot of time alone. I am a hiker, a camper, and a documentary filmmaker.

What goes around comes around.

Joshi from Calcutta, India :

Karma is a big thing in India. Whatever goes around comes around.

Almost thirty years ago, when I started my business of selling computer keyboards, I hired a very dynamic salesman. He was so good at promoting our products that within a period of five years, our sales quadrupled. I took good care of him with big bonuses, yearly promotions, and blind trust.

Eventually, he left to start his own company. He sold his house and other assets to get the seed money. He became my competitor. But within a few years, he lost everything and went bankrupt.

One day he came to my office and asked for forgiveness. It turned out that he was cheating me behind my back. For all the sales he made while working for me, he took a commission from the dealers. He received all this black money in cash, so we could not trace it. He invested this black money along with his personal assets into his business.

Kumar Anu: Did you forgive him?

My forgiveness will not remove his bad karma.

Give that you Seek.

Tarun from Hyderabad, India:

I met Raj on my first day at work. We had joined a telemarketing company after high school. Our job was to sell music players, and our income was the minimum wage. We could hardly make ends meet. The rent, the grocery, the clothes, the metro pass—it was impossible to survive on that income.

But, to my surprise, Raj donated ten percent of his salary every month. That implied that he was without food for three days. I could never understand his philosophy, and one day I decided to talk to him about it.

tribe, and agriculture was the only source of income. They did not have money, resources, or the modern amenities —but they were connected to the source of happiness.

That day I realized that happiness is a relative phenomenon. It's all about perception. It's inside your mind. And we can find happiness at a moment's notice.

Kumar Anu: And how do we find happiness at a moment's notice?

When you are unhappy, change your perception of happiness, because happiness arrives the way you define it.

If you think that buying an expensive car will bring you happiness —it will.

And if you think that breathing fresh air will bring you happiness —it will.

We don't have to change the scenery to be happy. We have to change the script.

Find your gifts.

Arun from Punjab, India:

Happiness is in using your God gifted talents.

As a child, I loved writing poetry. In my adolescent years, I loved writing essays about life. But at age eighteen, I had to kill my love for reading and writing.

I came from a family of engineers. My grandfather was a mechanical engineer, and my father was an electronics engineer. They loved designing and assembling things. They made a lot of money and were very respected in their fields.

After completing high school, I decided to pursue literature. But my family and friends convinced me that there is no money in literature. And after many discussions, I understood that if I pursue literature—I will never ever become rich, and I will regret my decision all my life. Hence, I decided to become a computer engineer to pursue a better life.

"Raj, in my opinion, you should start donating after a few years, when you earn more," I said.

"Tarun, if I cannot donate with my bare minimum income, I will always find excuses to donate when I earn millions," Raj replied.

His reply touched my soul, and I was transformed into a different person, right at that moment.

Kumar Anu: Did he inspire you to start donating?

It's been thirty years since I met Raj. We became business partners, started our own company, made good money, and we never stopped donating.

Live in the Moment.

Riku from Tokyo, Japan:

On my daughter's fifth birthday, I asked her what she wanted. She thought for a few moments and replied, "Papa, I want you on my birthday." At that time, I could not understand what she meant by her words.

My physical body was with my daughter, but my mind was someplace else—planning something, checking my social media status, or worrying about the future.

The biggest suffering in life happens when in the present moment, you want to be someplace else.

Have you ever wondered why kids are always happy? It is because they don't have a past and they cannot think about their future. They are peace within me. I found myself closer to almighty.

My parents and my in-laws tried to convince me, but I was adamant. This is my twentieth year in the ashram, and there is no place in the world like this.

Kumar Anu: Who takes care of your children? Don't you have a responsibility towards them?

My younger child stays with me in the ashram. He goes to the ashram school. My eldest child stays with his father in Mumbai. They come to visit me in the ashram.

Every child has to follow his own destiny. And my children are following their destiny.

For me, Happiness is all about dedicating your life to Almighty.

Om Shanti Shanti Shanti!

Embrace Change.

Donna, from New Jersey, USA:

I have always resisted change, but life has taught me to embrace change.

I lost my job during the global economic crisis. My job was my identify, my dignity, my life.

I had centered everything around my job. I bought my house a mile away from my workplace so that I don't waste my time in commute and spend more time with my children.

I did find a new job, but the problem was two hours of commute each way. This was very painful to accept—Wasting four hours on the train? Less time with my kids? Destroying my home life?

Because I had no choice, I accepted the new role

with resentment. I complained to God every day that how could he do this to me; but Almighty decided to ignore my request.

As life took over, after a few months, I stopped complaining. I accepted my train ride, made new friends on the train, and started writing a book that I had planned to write for many years. This commute gave me some 'me time' that was missing from my life. And in this process of embracing change—I found myself.

Kumar Anu: Do you plan to go back to your old life?

Only if Almighty wants me to embrace change one more time. For me, happiness is all about embracing change because when you embrace change, your inner conflict transforms into inner peace.

No pain. No gain.

Liam from Dublin, Ireland:

I grew up in a poor family. But my father, a truck driver, was very disciplined. In my teen years, he woke me up at four in the morning to load his truck. At five o' clock, I cooked my own food, and at six o' clock, I worked on my school assignments. If I did not get an A in any subject, he considered it an F.

It was very difficult to make him happy. I was tired of his rules and regulations, and I wanted to run away.

But little did I know that this discipline would ingrain the DNA of hard work within me.

When I decided to open my first food stall, I had no money, no training, and no employees. But I had always in the moment.

Life is all about experiences, and experiences exist only in the present moment.

Kumar Anu: Are you always in the present moment?

I practice hard to be in the present moment. When I talk with my daughter, I am there—totally there.

Compassion is the key.

Tapas from New Delhi, India:

For most of my life, I have been a selfish person. I grew up in urban India in the early seventies. There was scarcity all over the country, and I understood at a very early age that to be happy—I had to be merciless.

My parents bribed the government officials to get me into a better school with a full scholarship. We cheated our friends, in a land deal, to make additional money. We had excess stuff in our home, whereas, our neighbors survived on very basic amenities.

I always thought that this was the way to live in this cruel world.

But recently, I met an enlightened monk in the Himalayas, and his talks about compassion completely changed the perspective of my life.

I did not have the courage to listen to my heart.

As destiny had planned, I made a lot of money in my profession, but I was never happy. It was as if I was fighting with my inner nature, every day, to get things done. I felt that I was contaminating my soul.

At age forty, I started reading the Bible, the Quran, the Bhagavad Gita, and other Holy Books. To my surprise, I found that all the religious books clearly indicate that one should choose their profession as per their inner nature. Because if we are aligned with our inner nature, we will always find joy and happiness.

I was disheartened that the human race has not practiced the teachings imparted to us. Instead, we choose our professions based on greed.

I will never give that advice to my children.

Kumar Anu: What do your children do?

My daughter wants to pursue Art and my son wants to pursue Engineering. Their choices align with their inner nature.

It's all about Choices.

Sheetal from Chennai, India:

I got married when I was eighteen years old. It was an arranged marriage. I had my first child at the age of twenty and my second child at the age of twenty-one. My husband was good to me, and my children were adorable beings. My life was good on paper.

But, deep inside, I was very restless. It was as if I was following a script written by the society—show respect to your elders, be nice to your teachers, learn the house chores, get married, serve your husband, and serve your children. But, what about me? When do I get to take care of my needs? Where is my life?

When my eldest son was five years old, I left my family to join an ashram in southern India. The monastic community in the ashram brought deep the skill of hard work. I literally managed the entire place on my own—buying the groceries, cutting the vegetables, cooking the food, serving my customers, and cleaning the dishes. I did this continuously for two years.

Kumar Anu: I can see pride on your face. You are a self-made man.

My capacity to work hard paid off its dividends, and today I own multiple restaurants in Dublin, Ireland.

Find a reason to live.

Ajay from New Delhi, India:

My father had the soul of a mathematician. He was a professor of artificial intelligence at Delhi University. He was very popular among his students, and they called him the God of Math.

After retirement, he gave his life to Sudoku, a math-puzzle game. He would spend ten to twelve hours every day playing the game. He used to participate in Sudoku competitions all over the world.

At the age of sixty-five, he had a stroke and was in a coma with life-support treatment. The doctors lost all hope, and the family was asked to make a decision about letting him die. My son came up with the idea of solving a Sudoku puzzle in front of him before we sent him to the almighty. As we struggled to solve the puzzle, he rolled his eyes, he started moving his hands, and he gave us the final number that solved the puzzle. That game brought him back to life. He lived for another twenty years.

Kumar Anu: Amazing! It's the miracle of life.

His message was simple—it's our passion that keeps us alive. All we have to do is find it and enjoy it.

Happiness is dishwashing.

Maria from Phoenix, Arizona, USA:

Happiness is in dishwashing.

Yes, you heard it right. This simple, dull, and boring task has taught me a lot about happiness.

In fact, many other household tasks, like cleaning, cutting vegetables, or organizing closets, can help us to let go of any internal stress. The problem is that most of us consider these tasks to be boring, and hence we develop a lot of resistance around it.

The more we resist, the more we produce negative emotions.

I took up dishwashing as an exercise for letting go. However, it taught me a lot about life. I completely surrender when I wash the dishes—reducing the flow of water to the bare minimum, removing the grease from the plates with deep love, and finally putting the dishes in the dishwasher as a piece of art. I completely let go.

Kumar Anu: I can feel peaceful energy around you.

Often, I have had intuitive insights into life after washing the dishes. I have released physical and mental stress while doing the dishes. And most importantly, I have experienced limitless happiness.

Develop Mastery and Perfection.

Chef Tony from Italy:

There is only one road to success—and that is through the work you do and mastering the work you do. You keep on doing the same thing, again and again, until it becomes your second nature.

I am not a gifted chef. I have worked hard to reach my pinnacle. Twenty years ago, I ate one of the best caramel custard in Italy, and right there, I decided to give my life in making custards. The initial custards were terrible, but I did not lose hope.

I became obsessed with the custards. My mind was focused on making the best custard in the world. Sleeping, eating, working, or playing—all I did was devising methods to improve the custard. It took me five years to make the perfect caramel custard. Actually, you can say that I have done a Ph.D. in making custards. Today my restaurant is world famous because of my custards.

Kumar Anu: So, making caramel custards is the secret of your success?

No. The secret of my success is achieving perfection in whatever task I undertake. I give my heart and soul to it until it gets completed.

Happiness is your Work.

Daichi from Kyoto, Japan:

I am always Happy.

Kumar Anu: Sir, you are the first person in my research who has given me that answer. Can you tell me the secret of your happiness?

I am a sushi chef in Japan. I own and manage a small restaurant. There are only two employees—my wife and me. We don't make a lot of money, we work very hard, but we are very happy people.

I enjoy every moment in my restaurant—selecting the sushi, slicing the sushi, preparing the sushi, and then serving the sushi to the customers. I do my work with complete dedication, and this gives me happiness.

People think that happiness is dependent on the type of work they do. This perspective has destroyed the human race in recent times.

I have seen janitors enjoying their work because of dedication, and I have seen corporate executives disliking their work because of apathy. It does not matter what you do—but if you give one hundred percent to what you do, you will start enjoying life.

Here is the secret—fall in love with what you do, and you will find happiness.

Future has no Guarantees.

Rita from Miami, Florida, USA:

Today is my sixtieth birthday. For the last forty years, my husband and I have been saving twenty-five percent of our income in a retirement fund.

We are middle class people and have worked all our lives. We always did the right thing—we drove an old car, we did not take vacations, and we lived in a small house.

We wanted to have a secure retirement; hence, we planned for our future.

Kumar Anu: I see tears in your eyes. Is everything okay?

Last year we lost every dollar in our retirement fund. Our savings from the last forty years were wiped out in a day. A financial advisor was managing our retirement funds, and he invested in stock options that collapsed overnight.

We lost forty years of our life.

Kumar Anu: I feel your pain. There is a lot of learning in your story. Do you have a message for the younger people out there?

Enjoy the present moment. Save for the future, but do not depend on it—you never know what the future holds.

* * *

About the Author

Kumar Anu is an Author, Traveler and Philosopher. Through his books, he intends to help humanity find meaning and purpose. The word Moksha (Inner Freedom) became the essence of his life when he started practicing the teachings of the Bhagavad Gita.

Printed by Libri Plureos GmbH in Hamburg,
Germany